CONTENTS

THIS ANNUAL BELONGS TO...

_____

Published 2023.

Little Brother Books Ltd, Ground Floor,
23 Southernhay East, Exeter, Devon EX1 1QL

books@littlebrotherbooks.co.uk
www.littlebrotherbooks.co.uk

Printed in China. EU Address: Korte Leemstraat 3,
2018 Antwerpen, Belgium

WELCOME TO CRETACIA!

Cretacia is like one big, colourful playground to Rocky, Tiny, Bill and Mazu. Lakes, volcanoes, glaciers, jungle mazes and sticky swamps - you name it - the four friends just keep discovering more of this roar-some land!

EEEEEEEEEK!

In Cretacia there's a scary surprise waiting around almost every corner; from carnivorous plants to lava flows and everything in between! But the dinos have learned that being brave and working together goes a long way towards keeping them safe.

When the friends have finished adventuring for the day they can return to their cosy home for a good night's sleep. Complete with a dormitory, roof garden, garage and cosy beds, the Den has everything the dinos need to live in dino-fabulous style.

BOOM BOOM BOOM

By far the biggest, scariest and most mysterious of all the creatures in Cretacia is Giganto. He's rivalled only by Spinosaurus - a truly terrifying dino!

ALL ABOUT...
GIGANTOSAURUS!

GIGANTO

Giganto might look terrifying, but he has a gentle side. He's proved to be a friend to Rocky, Tiny, Bill and Mazu, often turning up to help them quicker than you can say, 'Big, scary dino'!

ROAAWR!

The four friends used to be very wary of Giganto, but after 'the big guy' helped them out of a few scrapes, they realised he could be trusted.

Giganto can be quite playful with the young dinos. He's been known to give them rides and flick them into the air with his tail!

Weeeeeeeeee!

Giganto's only true nemesis is Spinosaurus - bigger, meaner and scarier than Giganto in every way. One thing Spino doesn't have is friends to help him. Mazu once thought quickly to use crystals and water to melt ice that Spino was standing on and get him away from Giganto.

Life can be tiring for a big dino like Giganto. In the evening he likes nothing more than to visit his friends, then head home to his own cosy den for a good night's sleep.

DEN DIFFERENCES

The dinos are hanging out in the Den. Can you spot six differences in these two pictures? Colour in a dino footprint as you find each one.

ANSWERS ON PAGES 76-77

ALL ABOUT ROCKY...

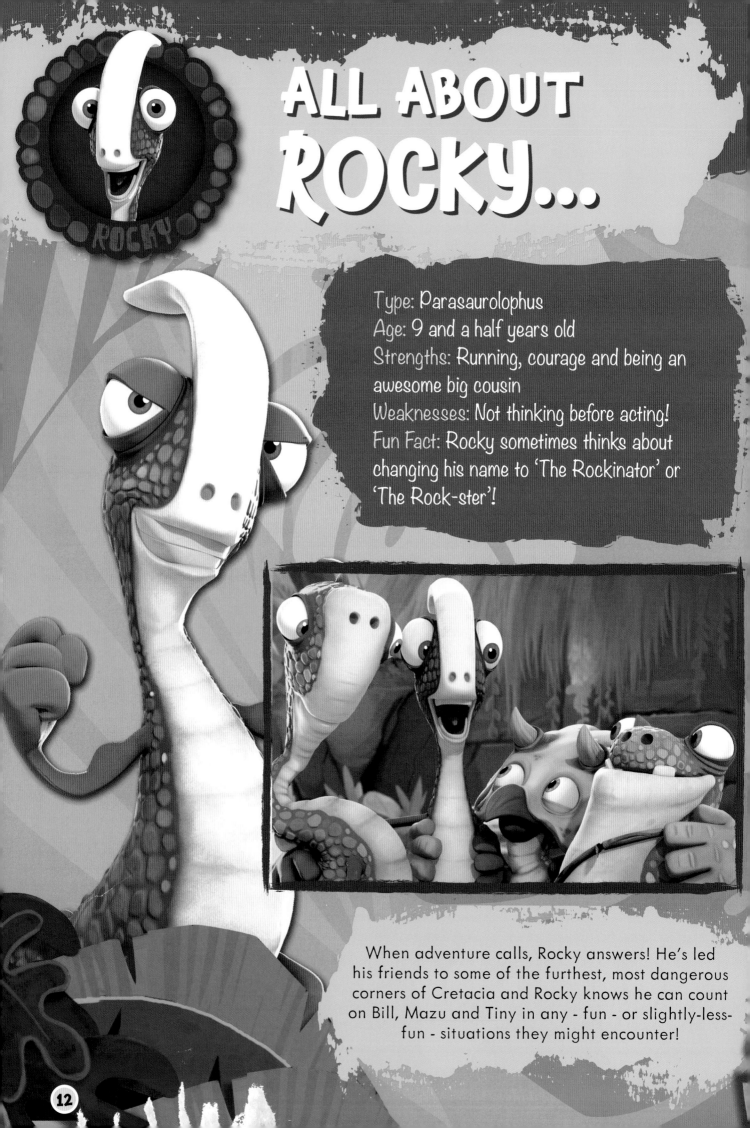

Type: Parasaurolophus
Age: 9 and a half years old
Strengths: Running, courage and being an awesome big cousin
Weaknesses: Not thinking before acting!
Fun Fact: Rocky sometimes thinks about changing his name to 'The Rockinator' or 'The Rock-ster'!

When adventure calls, Rocky answers! He's led his friends to some of the furthest, most dangerous corners of Cretacia and Rocky knows he can count on Bill, Mazu and Tiny in any - fun - or slightly-less-fun - situations they might encounter!

Rocky thinks Giganto is totally roar-some and will tell anyone who'll listen that they're best buds. He knows that although the gigantic dino looks fierce and terrifying, he's always there to help when Rocky and his friends are in trouble.

Rocky has been known to jump into situations head first, but he's learned that if he sticks with his friends things work out for the best.

...AND ROLO!

Rocky's tiny baby cousin, Rolo, is a cute little bundle of Parasaurolophus! He loves sleeping, his toy 'Snuggle-saurus' and most of all Rocky! Rolo hatched from an egg, which Rocky guarded, and his big cousin has been looking out for him ever since.

A NEW BEST T

ROCKY

The four friends were playing freeze tag on their own because Giganto wouldn't play with them. Just as they needed a roar to unfreeze them, a new dino came along and roared loudly. Rocky was impressed.

WOW!

I'm T Rex. My friends call me Rex, you can call me T.

The dinos played some games with T: T Rex freeze tag, basketball and T-tug-of-war and he won every time. Tiny, Mazu and Bill got tired of watching T show off and they went home.

I won!

Giganto, Gi-schmanto - I'm the greatest!

Rocky told his new 'Best T' about Giganto: the biggest, toughest scariest dino in all of Cretacia. T was jealous.

No one's than Gig

T suggested an idea for a mean new game: tying a string of coconuts to Giganto's tail while he was asleep so he'd be spooked when he woke up. T thought he'd be so embarrassed that he'd leave Cretacia forever.

Rocky was shocked. He told T that he'd never do that to his friend Giganto, and that friends should be kind and look out for each other.

We've got your back Rocky!

Just then Rocky's friends appeared.

So T tried to trick Giganto without Rocky's help, but the little dino chased after him...

Leave my friend alone!

ROARRR!

...ke up Giganto!

As T ran away, Rocky and his friends fell into the river and started to float towards the waterfall!

Eeeek!

WOOOSH!

Luckily, Giganto moved a log into their path and saved them.

SNORE!

Giganto won't stop freeze tag with a roar but he'll stop it with a snore!

Safely back on dry land Rocky reflected that Giganto might not always want to play but he was always looking out for them.

17

COOL CROSSWORD

Use the picture clues to fill out the crossword.
Tick the words off as you find each one.

HINT
the words are names of some of your favourite dinos!

ROCKY

DOWN

2 ☐ 3 ☐ 5 ☐

1 | | 2 R | | |

3

4 | | I | |

5

6 M | | | | | | | |

ACROSS

1 ☐ 4 ☐ 6 ☐

ANSWERS ON PAGES 76–77

DINO DOTS

Create a picture of Rocky by joining the dots then colour him in with some roar-inspiring reds!

GIGANTIC ADVENTURE

Can you find the details in this picture of the dino friends on an adventure? Tick them off as you spot each one.

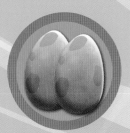

ALL ABOUT... THE CARTS!

Mazu invented these dino-tastic carts for her and her friends to fly, swim and speed around Cretacia. Read on to find out more.

TINY TRIKE

The Tiny Trike reflects Tiny's love of colour. If she pulls a lever, colourful sparkles shoot out the back!

MAZMOBILE

The Mazmobile's wings allow Mazu to fly super-fast to anywhere in Cretacia.

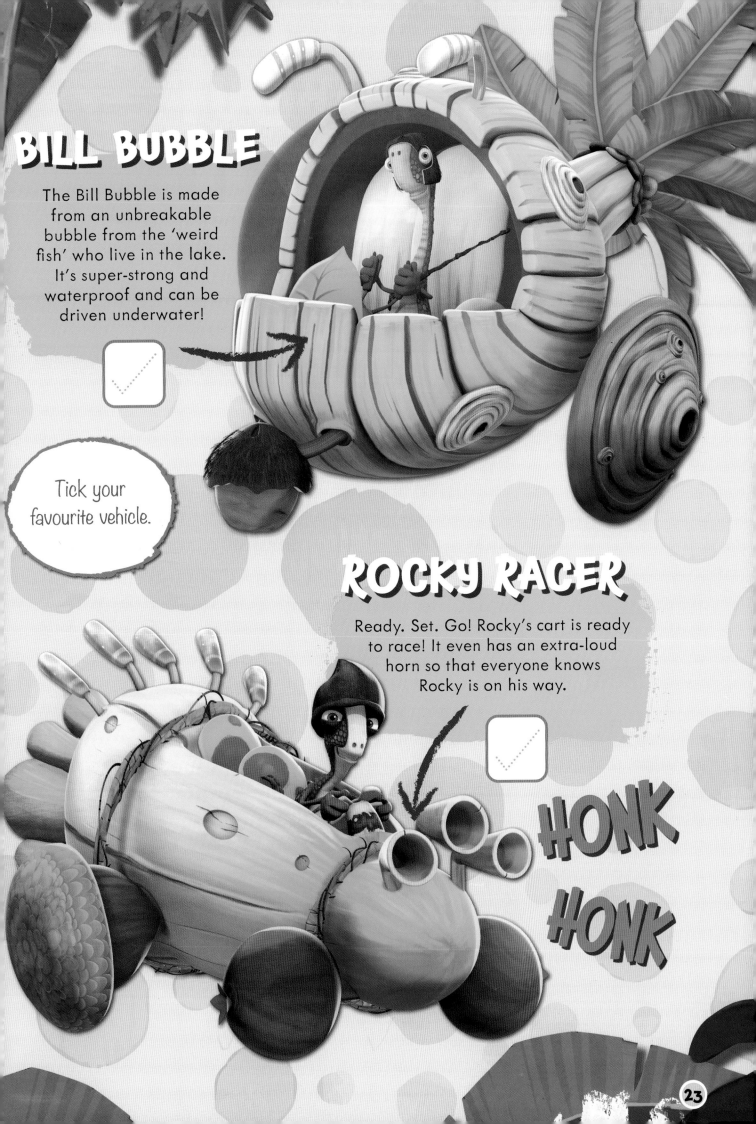

BILL BUBBLE

The Bill Bubble is made from an unbreakable bubble from the 'weird fish' who live in the lake. It's super-strong and waterproof and can be driven underwater!

Tick your favourite vehicle.

ROCKY RACER

Ready. Set. Go! Rocky's cart is ready to race! It even has an extra-loud horn so that everyone knows Rocky is on his way.

HONK

HONK

ALL ABOUT MAZU...

Type: Ankylosaurus
Age: 9 and a half years old
Strengths: Brains and inventing skills
Weaknesses: Getting into sticky situations in the name of science!
Fun Fact: Mazu's tail club is super-strong and can be used as a tool to break things!

Mazu's super-inventive and has built some awesome creations for her friends including crystal powered jet packs and a rocket designed to fly to the moon!

Mazu loves exploring and trying to understand the world around her, but sometimes she's thinking so much about a discovery that she doesn't notice the danger!

Rocky, Tiny and Bill know they can count on Mazu as a friend. Her inventions have solved more problems than they can count and made for some really cool adventures.

...AND ZAK!

Mazu's little brother Zak may look super sweet but he's quite a handful. When Mazu attempted to babysit for Zak and the other babies she had her work cut out for her!

COCONUTS FOR COCOPHONES

Mazu creates an amazing invention but runs
into problems when it becomes too popular!

Mazu is showing her friends a cool new invention - the
coco-phone! 'They're made from coconuts and you can use it to
talk to dinos who are far away,' Mazu explained. She pointed
to an antenna on top of a bamboo tower. 'That helps it transmit
your voice from one cocophone to another!'

Mazu gave cocophones to all of her friends in Cretacia and everyone loved them -
everyone except Giganto. 'He's a dino of few words,' she told her friends, 'but maybe
he'll talk to me on one of these.' She tried to give the big dino a phone but sadly for
Mazu he didn't take one.

Meanwhile, Patchy and Dillo found a cocophone. 'Snack time,' said Dillo, lifting it to his mouth. 'Hello,' said the Cocophone, causing Dillo to drop the phone in shock. 'That sounds like Mazu - Mazu turned into a coconut!' The phone landed in front of a carnivorous plant, who gobbled it up!

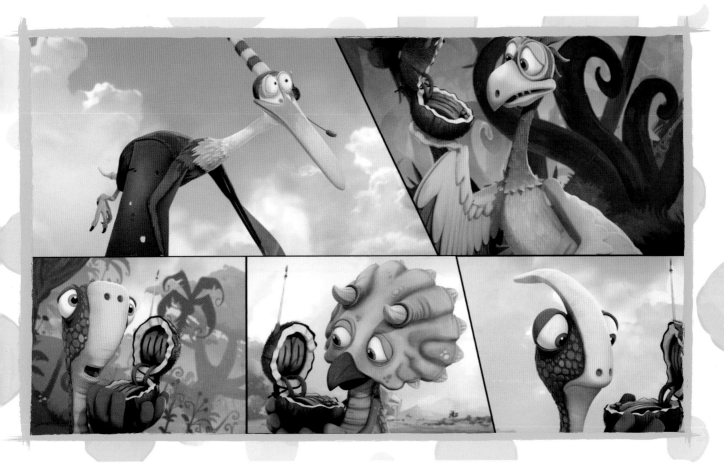

Archie found Dillo and Patchy running around in panicky circles. 'The plant's eaten Mazu!' cried Dillo. Archie used a cocophone to call his friends. 'Mazu needs our help!' he told them. 'Don't worry Mazu, we'll save you!' exclaimed Rocky.

Mazu noticed that the antenna tower was shaking because so many people were using their cocophones at the same time. 'I'd better fix that,' said Mazu, worried. She climbed up the tower but it fell over, leaving Mazu stuck, dangling so high up in the air that even Giganto couldn't reach her.

Meanwhile, Tiny, Bill and Rocky had gathered by the carnivorous plant to try to make it spit out Mazu. Tiny tickled the plant and it spat out not Mazu but a cocophone! 'Mazu needs your help at the tower!' boomed a strange, deep voice over the phone.

The friends flew to the tower on Archie's back and used a vine to make a zip wire, so that Mazu could slide safely to the ground. She told the others that it was Giganto whose voice they'd heard. 'He wouldn't speak *to* me on the cocophone,' she smiled, 'but at least he spoke *for* me!'

Later, Mazu gathered her friends together. 'I'm sorry for pushing my cocophones so hard,' she said. 'To make it up to you I have a present for everyone.' She revealed a large pile of coconuts. 'More phones?' asked Rugo. 'No,' Mazu laughed. 'These are just coconuts - the eating kind!'

CRETACIAN COLOURING

The four best friends are playing a game. Give them some bright colours to help them win!

MAZE RACE

Rocky, Bill, Tiny and Mazu are racing through the maze to Giganto's Den. Follow the trails to find out who wins!

A

B

C

D

FINISH

DINO DOOR HANGER

Make this roar-some hanger for your bedroom door!

Don't want to cut up your book? Ask an adult to photocopy or scan and print this page.

1. Carefully cut along the dotted lines. Always ask an adult for help with using scissors.
2. Now fold your door hanger in half and stick it together with stick glue.
3. Colour in and add your name to the back of the door hanger.
4. Your creation is ready to hang on your bedroom door!

DON'T WAKE UP THE DINOSAUR!

FOLD

_____ 'S
ROOM

CRAZY CARTS

VROOOOM! Make like Mazu and invent your very own dino cart. Answer the questions, then draw your creation in the space opposite.

MY CART IS CALLED:

....

HINT
Try writing your name then adding one of these words: 'mobile', 'trike', 'racer' or 'bike', or create your own speedy-sounding name!

MY CART IS MADE OF:

....

HINT
Why not choose something that can be found in Cretacia like leaves, sticks, flowers, walnuts or rocks.

MY CART HAS:

....

HINT
Does your cart have any cool features like a horn or leaf propellers?

MY CART CAN:

....

HINT
Can your cart do something special like fly or go underwater?

Draw your own cool
creation here.

For more
inspiration check out
the dino friends' carts on
pages 22-23.

ALL ABOUT TINY...

Type: Triceratops
Age: 9 years old
Strengths: Her Triceratops-strength, being artistic and telling funny jokes!
Weaknesses: Sometimes Tiny's dreamy, artistic nature can get her into scrapes - luckily her friends are always there to help.
Fun Fact: Triceratops usually love mud baths but Tiny hates them - yuck!

Tiny's positivity and creative-thinking make her the perfect friend to have on an adventure. She's a loyal, kind friend to Rocky, Bill and Mazu and an all-round dino-shaped bundle of fun!

Artistic Tiny is always finding canvases for her art - rocks, leaves, cave walls - she'd even paint on Giganto if she could! She's most happy when she's mixing up bright coloured paints to paint dino-tastic portraits of her friends.

Triceratops are super-strong dinos, but Tiny has no interest in uprooting trees or being a warrior like her big brother, Trey. Tiny thinks picking flowers, dancing and telling jokes is far more fun.

...AND TORI!

Tiny's baby sister Tori (or 'Tori Dinosaur-y' as Tiny likes to call her) is as silly and fun as her big sister. She's even a budding artist like her too! Tori adores Tiny and her big brother Trey, who are always there to play games or sing silly songs when she needs them.

SINGOSAURUS

It's Tiny's dream to perform her song at the Taste of Cretacia food festival – but first she has to help two dinos overcome their differences.

Tiny and her friends were practising her song for the Taste of Cretacia food festival that night. It was a song about friendship, with Iggy and Tiny's brother Trey performing a duet. 'That sounds great!' cried Tiny. 'It sure does,' replied Trey, 'and it'll sound even better when Iggy gets here.'

When Iggy arrived he didn't look very well. 'Cough, cough! I've got a dino-sore throat,' he complained. The friends sent him home to rest and Tiny tried to figure out how to replace him. 'My song's about friendship,' she said. 'It won't be the same without two friends singing it!'

38

Just then the friends spotted Totor and Cror hovering suspiciously near a pile of food. 'We weren't stealing, we...' Cror thought quickly. 'We want to try out for the band!' Tiny was so impressed with Cror's audition that she asked her to perform with Trey at the food festival, but the raptor and Trey didn't like each other. 'With him? No way!' said Cror. 'Wait... did you say *food* festival?'

During rehearsals Cror and Trey started arguing. Mazu had to build two separate stages for them, but Trey still wasn't happy. 'Her stage is higher than mine!' he complained. Mazu made the stages higher, but Cror said that her stage was too high and that she was afraid of heights. 'You're impossible!' humphed Trey.

Cror stomped off to the grotto, closely followed by
Trey and Tiny. Inside the cave Cror and Trey carried
on arguing and their voices echoed outside, waking up
Giganto who was sleeping nearby. He moved and the
rocks for the stage wobbled and fell in front of
the entrance to the cave!

Tiny was disappointed. 'It's been my dream to play my song at this festival,' she said
forlornly. 'But I guess my dream won't come true now. It's all been for nothing.' Trey
and Cror were sorry. 'No Sis, not for nothing,' said Trey. The two dinos knew what to
do - they started to sing their song to Tiny.

The others could hear the singing from outside the cave. When Giganto heard it he started to dance! He stomped his big, heavy feet in time to the music and made the ground shake, moving the rocks that were blocking the entrance. 'We're free!' cried Tiny.

Tiny spoke to Cror and Trey. 'If you can sing in harmony, can you live in harmony too?' she said. 'I'm sorry I've been so grumpy,' said Trey. 'Well, I've been acting pretty bossy - even for me,' apologised Cror. Later, the band performed their song for the festival, as their Cretacian friends clapped and cheered.

DINO DOODLES

Make like Tiny and test your artistic skills. Follow the instructions to create your own epic drawing of Cretacia!

TINY

Add some green leaves and tasty walnuts to the top of this tree.

Colour these flowers for Tiny to pick.

DINO BATTLE

Rooaaarr!! Giganto and Spinosaurus are having a fight. Decide the winner by giving them marks out of 10 on the scoring cards.

Giganto's keen sense of smell and sharp teeth make him a fearsome predator.

FIGHT FACT

Giganto once used his feet to break some ice under Spino's feet. The big bully fell down a rock face and stomped off in defeat!

Giganto's small arms aren't much use in fights - or for scratching his back!

Giganto and Spino both have powerful tails that they can use to move big objects or to fight.

THUD THUD

Giganto has the ability to make friends and work as a team.

GIGANTOSAURUS

GIGANTO SCORES

SIZE	/10
STRENGTH	/10
FIERCENESS	/10
INTELLIGENCE	/10
TEAMWORK	/10
TOTAL	/50

FIGHT FACT

Spino once made rocks fall in front of Giganto's Den, causing him to be stuck inside. Luckily, some of the dino's friends were able to help set him free.

SPINO SCORES

SIZE	/10
STRENGTH	/10
FIERCENESS	/10
INTELLIGENCE	/10
TEAMWORK	/10
TOTAL	/50

Spino is a lean, mean eating machine, who will stop at nothing to get what he wants - or pick fights with Giganto!

If the wind catches Spino's sail-like back plate it could cause him to topple over!

ROOOOAAARRR!!!

Spino can be easily distracted and has been outwitted by Giganto.

Spino is perhaps the bigger of these two huge dinos.

SPINOSAURUS

THE WINNER IS...

ALL ABOUT BILL...

Type: Brachiosaurus

Age: 7 years old

Strengths: Cooking, singing and his long neck - perfect for looking out for scary dinos!

Weaknesses: Getting scared - a lot!

Fun Fact: :Bill once accidentally scared meanie raptors Totor and Cror into thinking he was the 'Harvest Monster' when a pumpkin lantern got stuck on his head!

When Bill isn't jetting about in the Bill Bubble, he can be found eating, cooking, sleeping - or hiding behind the nearest rock when a scary dino's around!

Bill loves food and can often be found chowing down on delicious Cretacian coconuts, berries and fruit. He's also a great cook and wows his friends with dishes like his 'world-famous' pumpkin bread made from pumpkin goo - yum!

This timid dino has shown that he's 'Capa-Bill' of being brave when it comes to helping his friends. Bill once saved Leon from fast-flowing lava by swooping him up into the air with is jet pack.

...AND LEENA!

Bill's cute little sister Leena is full of energy and loves hanging out with the other babies Tori, Rolo and Zak. She's just as much of a food fan as Bill and gobbles up his berry smoothies.

BILL

PLINK, PLONK AND PLUNK

One day, while playing at the lake the dinos met some new friends.

We swam up the river looking for adventure!

I'm Plink!

I'm Plunk!

I'm Plonk!

The dinos and Plink, Plonk and Plunk started playing together, but Bill found it hard to join in.

He didn't like water-skiing.

He couldn't control his bubble.

... and he put on his snorkelling mask back to front.

Bill felt left out, but he had an idea - he'd have a picnic with Giganto.

If the new kids see me hanging out with Giganto they'll definitely want to play with me.

But, as Bill was looking for food in the picnic basket, Giganto's tail caught hold of the handle and he carried Bill into the lake...

... and dropped him right next to Termy!

Gulp, you're not Giganto!

And I'm not your friend!

UNDERWATER ADVENTURE

Help Bill find his friend Plunk at the end of this underwater maze. Collect lily pads and avoid obstacles like spiky coral and terrifying Termy, who is hiding down one of the paths!

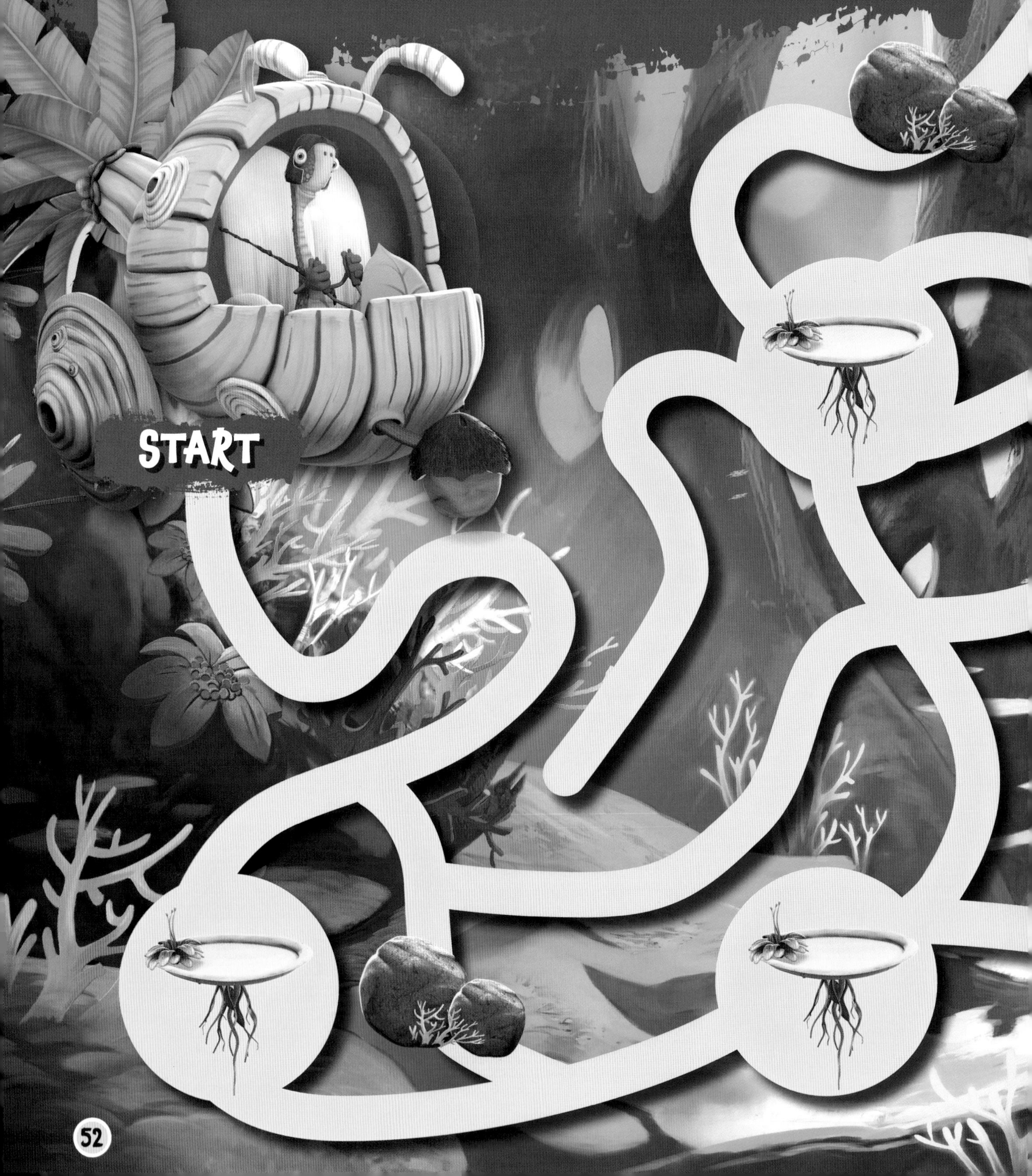

START

52

END

How many lily pads did you collect? Write the number in the box.

CUTE CONUNDRUM

Bill, Rocky, Mazu and Tiny love hanging out with the baby dinos. Can you spot the odd one out in each row?

1

A B C D

2

A B C D

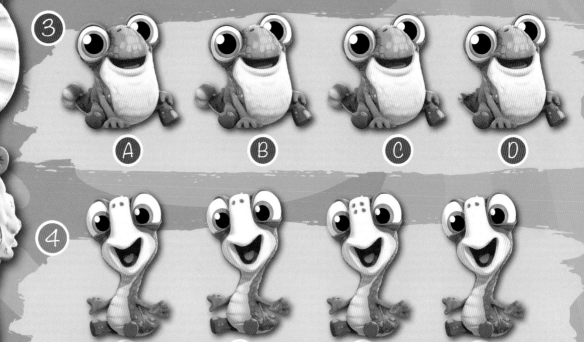

3

A B C D

4

A B C D

ANSWERS ON PAGES 76-77

SIBLING SILLINESS

Things can get a little crazy when you're babysitting these cuties. Label the jumbled pieces of this picture to put them into the correct order.

A B C D E F G H

		H				A	

WHICH DINO ARE YOU?

Take this quiz to find out!

Do you like science?

NO

YES

Are you good at painting and drawing?

YES

NO

Are you good at staying focussed?

NO

YES

Do you like making discoveries and inventing things?

NO

Are you often positive and happy

YES

YES

MAZU

Like Mazu, you love to study the world and have an unstoppable drive to work out how things tick! With the help of your friends you might just make that big discovery!

TINY

You're artistic and creative like Tiny. Sometimes you get lost looking at the world around you, but with your positive attitude you always come out on top.

START

Are you confident if you have to speak in front of your class at school?

NO

Are you nervous when you meet new people?

YES

NO

YES

If you see something scary do you hide?

NO

Are you good at sports?

NO

NO

YES

Can you smell lunch a mile off?

YES

Would you choose a picnic over an adventure?

NO

NO

Do you sometimes act before you think?

NO

YES

YES

YES

BILL

Sometimes you're a little nervous like Bill, but you're kind and thoughtful and can be brave when it comes to helping your friends.

ROCKY

You're always on the lookout for adventure and sometimes get into sticky situations. If you're lucky like Rocky, though, you have good friends who look out for you!

ALL ABOUT...
DINO FRIENDS!

Meet the dinos' Cretacian buddies. From friendly fish to flightless birds, the dinos love hanging out with these colourful friends.

TREY

The dinos all look up to Trey who's brave and strong and one of the 'Guardians of the Herd', who protect the creatures of Cretacia. He also has a sensitive side and is a fun big brother to Tiny and Tori.

LEON

Turtle-like Leon is amphibious, which means he can walk on land or swim underwater! He's quite slow on land (and has had to be rescued from fast-flowing lava!). He's a kind and thoughtful friend and can be found helping the dinos on their adventures or swimming in the lake where he lives.

TERMY

Termy or 'The Terminator' isn't exactly friendly and the dinos used to avoid her at all costs! But when she got stuck in the frozen land, the four friends helped her to return. Since then she's a little kinder to the dinos - but she still finds them annoying when they disturb her afternoon naps!

PLINK, PLONK, PLUNK.

Plink, Plonk and Plunk are a kind of Cretacian dolphin or ichthyosaur. The dinos find them playful and friendly and love playing hide and seek with them in their lake home.

59

ARCHIE

Archie is a flightless bird who wishes he could fly! He's often nervous and alert to danger which makes him the perfect babysitter or lookout.

RUGO

Rugo is a sort-of giant mouse, or Rugosodon, with strong back legs for jumping and big cheeks for storing food! She loves hanging out with the dinos and her other Rugosodon friends.

MARSHALL

Marshall (a.k.a. Marsh) is younger than the four dinos but much bigger than them. The young stegosaurus loves playing ball games and making lemonade for his dino friends.

AYATI

Ayati is a wise old brachiosaurus (like Bill - but huge!) She's very wise and likes to tell the young dinos about her life and offer advice when needed. She can be really fun too - Rocky has used her long neck as a slide!

HEGAN

Responsible and brave, Hegan is another 'Guardian of the Herds'. The pterosaur swoops in to sort out any danger and has given the dino friends a lift on her back!

SUPER SKETCHES

Complete these pictures of the four dino friends,
then colour them in with your brightest pens!

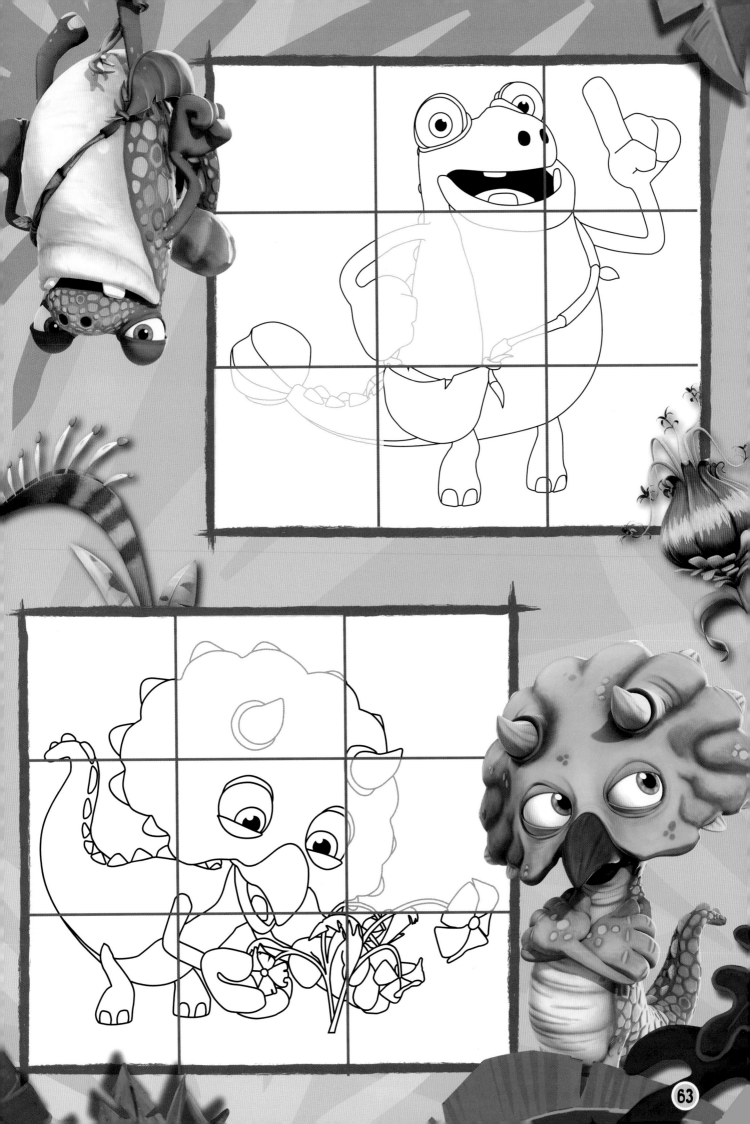

DINO QUIZ

How much do you know about the world of Giganto? Try this fun quiz to find out!

1

Who's the dino's biggest, scariest friend?

a) Hugeosaurus

b) Gigantosaurus

c) Trey

2

What is Rocky best at?

a) Running

b) Swimming

c) Sleeping

3

What does Mazu like doing?

a) Talking to Spinosaurus

b) Eating

c) Inventing things

4

What's the name of this friendly dino?

a) Marshall

b) Ayati

c) Mayati

5

Where do the dinos live?

a) Gigantoland

b) Cretacia

c) Jurassica

64

6

What is Bill's cart called?

a) The Speedy Submarine ☐
b) The Billmobile ☐
c) The Bill Bubble ☐

7

What are the names of these baddies?

a) Totor and Cror ☐
b) Simon and Ben ☐
c) Gater and Roar ☐

8

What does Tiny love doing?

a) Painting ☐
b) Rolling in mud ☐
c) Cooking ☐

9

Who is Giganto's biggest enemy?

a) T Rex ☐
b) Spinosaurus ☐
c) Rocky ☐

10

What kind of creatures are Plink, Plunk and Plonk like?

a) Whales ☐
b) Orcas ☐
c) Dolphins ☐

HOW MANY DID YOU GET RIGHT?

1-3: Good effort!

4-5: Dino-tastic! You're making progress on your dino discovery

6-10: You're a Gigantosaurus master!

ALL ABOUT... THE BADDIES!

Cretacia is home to some real meanies - from speedy raptors to gigantic predators. Meet some of them here... if you dare!

ROOOOAAARRR!!!

SPINOSAURUS

Spinosaurus is the biggest, deadliest dino in all of Cretacia. He's a match for Giganto in size and ferociousness and is not a fussy eater - he'll eat whatever or whoever gets in his way!

T REX

T Rex or T for short is a tough teenage dino and a bit of a show off. He thinks he's as scary as Giganto, but Rocky, Tiny, Mazu and Bill don't agree!

THUD
THUD
THUD

TOTOR AND CROR

These two raptor siblings can be mean to little dinos, but luckily the four friends always seem to get the better of them.

A SPLASH OF COLOUR

The dino friends are hanging out by the lake.
Join the fun by colouring them in!

FOLLOW THE FOOTPRINTS

Rocky is looking for his friends. Help him find them by following the pattern shown below.

START

FINISH

ANSWERS ON PAGES 76-77

MEMORY TEST

Look at this picture for three minutes then test your memory by answering the questions on the next page.

MEMORY TEST

What can you remember about the picture?
Test your memory with these questions.

1

How many waterfalls did you spot?
a) Ten ☐
b) One ☐
c) Two ☐

2

What does the sky look like in the picture?
a) Blue ☐
b) Black ☐
c) Red ☐

3

What is Rocky sitting on?
a) A leaf ☐
b) A rock ☐
c) Giganto ☐

4

What is Bill doing?
a) Eating ☐
b) Running ☐
c) Waving ☐

5

What is Mazu holding?
a) Her brother Zak ☐
b) A magnifying glass ☐
c) A book ☐

6

What is Tiny doing?
a) Waving ☐
b) Painting ☐
c) Dancing ☐

7

How many orange flowers did you count?
a) Four ☐
b) Seven ☐
c) Two ☐

8

Where were the dinos hanging out?
a) At the Glacier ☐
b) By the Lake ☐
c) In the Jungle ☐

ANSWERS ON PAGES 76–77

CRACK THE CODE

Who's the friends' favourite dino?
Find out by using the key to spell out the answer.

A 	**B** 	**C** 	**D** 	**E** 	**F** 
G 	**H** 	**I** 	**J** 	**K** 	**L** 
M 	**N** 	**O** 	**P** 	**Q** 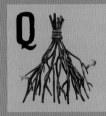	**R** 
S 	**T** 	**U** 	**V** 	**W** 	**X** 
Y 	**Z** 				

What do Rocky, Tiny, Mazu and
Bill think of Giganto?
Break the dino code to find out.

_____ _____ _____ _____ _____ _____

_____ _____ _____ _____ _____ _____ _____

ANSWERS ON PAGES 76–77

WIN A GIGANTOSAURUS ACTION FIGURE BUNDLE

Get ready for a ROARSOME adventure...

You can now stomp out all your favourite dino adventures at home with Rocky, Bill, Tiny, Mazu, and the **HUMUNGOUS** Gigantosaurus. These fun characters from the epic TV series are available now as super-cool action figures.

Enter our competition for a chance to win a **ROARING, STOMPING** Action Giganto! He's so fearsome with his amazing stomping and chomping movements and light-up spine.

ACTION GIGANTO

The lucky winner will also get their claws on **ALL SIX Gigantosaurus Buddies Mini Figures**. Each pack comes with a new 12cm prehistoric friend to find.

That's not all... Five runners-up can also kickstart their Gigantosaurus toy collection, with **three Buddies Mini Figures!**

BUDDIES MINI FIGURES

ENTER NOW FOR A CHANCE TO WIN.

SPOT THE DINO DIFFERENCES AND WIN!

How many differences can you spot?

Once you think you've found them all, fill in your answer at **www.GigantosaurusToys.co.uk** for your chance to win this dino-mite prize bundle.

ANSWERS

PAGES 10-11 - DEN DIFFERENCES

PAGES 18-19 - COOL CROSSWORD

PAGE 20-21 - GIGANTIC ADVENTURE

PAGE 32 - MAZE RACE

PAGE 52-53 - UNDERWATER ADVENTURE

There are seven lily pads to collect.

PAGE 54 - CUTE CONUNDRUM

1. C
2. B
3. D
4. C

PAGE 55 - SIBLING SILLINESS

PAGE 64-65 - DINO QUIZ

1. b
2. a
3. c
4. b
5. b
6. c
7. a
8. a
9. b
10. c

PAGE 70 - FOLLOW THE FOOTPRINTS

PAGE 71-72 - MEMORY TEST

1. c
2. a
3. b
4. c
5. c
6. b
7. a
8. c

PAGE 73 - CRACK THE CODE

The symbols spell: 'We love Giganto'

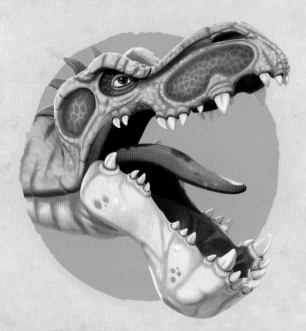